IT'S RAINING CATS AND FROGS

Marguérite Turnley

To order additional copy of this book, contact:
2708 Armidale Road Blaxland's Creek
 New South Wales 2460 Australia
info@shrubspublishing.com

IT'S RAINING CATS AND FROGS

It was raining every day and Raina couldn't go outside to play. She was feeling very cross. Tom kept making a fuss and she wanted to tell him to stop. But he was only a baby and didn't understand. "Tom," she said, in her best grown up voice, "If you keep yelling, I'm going to turn the TV up loud so I can't hear you."

Tom stopped crying and looked at her. He grinned. He didn't have any teeth yet but his grin made Raina grin too. Then he hit himself in the eye with his fist and began to cry again. "Wah, wah, wah."

"That's such a silly sound," said Raina. "I can make a better sound than that."

Raina began to rub her dry eyes and pretend to cry. She said, "Boo hoo, boo hoo." Then she looked at Tom and saw him watching her. He was quiet and when she rubbed her eyes, he copied her. When she rubbed her head, he rubbed his head. When she stamped her feet he tried to stamp his feet. He was lying in a baby bouncer and his feet couldn't reach the floor. Then he started crying again. He wanted so much to be like his big sister. He wanted to do everything she did.

All day it rained as usual but when it stopped after lunch

Raina put on her yellow plastic raincoat and hat. She put on her yellow gumboots and went out into the garden. She loved it when the rain stopped. All the trees dripped water, the grass squelched and the mud stuck to her boots. It was lovely.

Then she noticed the tank was overflowing. She knew mum was busy so she went over to see the water flowing. Down it came, like a shower. She watched it for a while and then stood under the water. It ran down over her yellow hat and dripped down onto her boots. "This is fun," she said. "It's like a real shower."

Raina jumped in fright when she heard a funny croaking

sound. She looked up and saw a frog sitting at the top of the tank watching her. It was a little green frog with big popping eyes. It was wet like her and shiny too. The frog blinked. Then it blinked again and it hopped down off the tank and landed on Raina's head. She tipped her head. It fell off and landed in her hand. It was very slippery. Its legs were long and its feet were webbed.

"Knee deep," said the frog. "What are you doing here little girl?"

"I'm taking a shower you silly frog. Don't you know anything?"

"Not much. I can see there's a shower. I can see you're all wet, like me."

Raina came out from under the water and sat on a log. She shook her head and drops of water sprinkled through the air. She wiped water from her eyes with her free hand and asked, "what's your name?"

"Letty. What's your name?"

"Raina. Are you a girl frog or a boy frog?"

"I'm a girl. Don't you know anything?" Letty laughed.

"I know a lot of things but I'm not telling you, " said Raina.

"I don't want to know anyway. I'm a happy frog. I like me

just as I am."

"Letty is a funny name for a frog. What does it mean?"

"It means I'm green and I like to sit on lettuce leaves in the garden."

"Why do you sit on lettuce leaves?"

"Since I'm green it's a good place for me to hide and I can catch insects with my tongue.   It's very long and sticky you see. I'm very good at it." Letty Frog stuck out her tongue.

"Yuck," said Raina. "That's rude. I'm not allowed to poke out my tongue. Mum says flies land on it and they taste horrible."

"I like flies. They're yummy. But I'm a frog you see," said Letty. "Sticking out my tongue is my way of catching dinner. And very tasty it is too."

"Oh. Well then, you must do it," agreed Raina. "I don't like eating insects. A beetle flew into my mouth the other day. He got lost in our kitchen. He tasted funny and I spat him out. He buzzed and flew out the door as fast as he could."

"That's good. He wouldn't have liked to be eaten. It isn't nice."

"Did someone try to eat you?"

"Yes. Have you got a cat?"

"Yes, his name is Sammy. He's black and white. He's fast too."

"Well, he tried to eat me yesterday but I jumped up on top of the tank. I've been there hiding from him all night. It's nice up there, and safe. Your cat can't climb up there. It's too high for him but I can spring up anywhere."

"He's inside in front of the fire now. He's sleeping."

"Good. Keep him there will you. It's not nice to be chased. I met an earwig the other day. He was hiding from the magpies. They wanted him for dinner. He thought he could hide on my lettuce leaf but I found him. He was sitting in my favourite spot."

"What did you do, Letty? Were you a naughty frog?"

"I tried to eat him of course. He was too quick for me though. He got away."

"You shouldn't be mean to earwigs, Letty. They have a right to live too."

"That's true, Raina. I didn't think of that. I only wanted to lie on my favourite lettuce leaf in the rain and have a bit of lunch. I didn't get any though. It rains a lot in winter. It's just the right time of year for frogs. We like the rain."

"I like winter too, Letty. I like hot chocolate and warm fires.

I like sitting on my chair watching TV and eating bananas when they're yellow and slippery."

"I'm green and slippery. Will I do?" Letty laughed.

"I don't want to eat you, silly. You're a nice green frog and but you wouldn't taste nice. I don't want to peel you or put you in a sandwich with sugar."

Raina grinned at Letty. "I've got an idea. Would you like to meet my little brother? Tom is only a baby but he would like to meet you. He likes frogs."

"He likes frogs, huh? Does he like to eat frogs?"

"No, silly. He likes to look at frogs. He likes to play with frogs. He doesn't talk much but he will probably talk to you. You sound the same as him when he has been crying. All croaky and funny."

"Lead the way, Raina. I'd like to meet your little brother who likes frogs."

Raina kept Letty gently in her hand and went to the back door. She hid her from Mum who was cooking lunch. She kept her safe from Sammy the cat who was waking up and stretching in front of the fire.

Tom bumped up and down in his bouncer and grinned at Raina. He couldn't talk yet but she knew he wanted to know

Raina. He couldn't talk yet but she knew he wanted to know what was in her hand. She knew he wanted to touch whatever she had. He didn't have to ask. She knew.

Tom put out his hand and Raina put Letty into his tiny white palm. Tom squealed and dropped Letty who leapt away and landed on the dining room table. She knocked over a vase of flowers and the glass broke. She jumped up onto the window ledge and sat waiting for the roof to fall in.

Raina and Tom's mum came in and said, "What's going on in here, Raina. Why is Tom squealing?"

Tom stopped then and grinned at Raina. Mum just stood in

the doorway and waited as Raina tried to think of something to say. Then the worst thing happened. Letty jumped onto Mum's head and sat in her hair.

He hung on tight with his webbed feet while Raina's mum jumped and tried to get the frog out of her hair. Mum squealed like Tom.

Raina and Tom laughed and laughed. They laughed until they cried. Their new friend Letty jumped out of mum's hair and out the door. Sammy the cat ran out the door too but he was too late. The frog was quick and he escaped. He wasn't going to be anyone's dinner. Not that little slippery green frog.

The End.